Your Dad, My Mum

Hazel Townson

Your Dad, My Mum

RED FOX

For my most supportive writer friends,
Sherry Ashworth and Beverley Hughesden

A Red Fox Book
Published by Random House Children's Books
20 Vauxhall Bridge Road, London SW1V 2SA

A division of The Random House Group Limited
London Melbourne Sydney Auckland
Johannesburg and agencies throughout the world

First published in Great Britain by The Bodley Head 2000

This edition published by Red Fox, 2001

3 5 7 9 10 8 6 4

Copyright © Hazel Townson 2000
Red Fox edition 2001

Printed and bound in Denmark by
Nørhaven

Papers used by Random House are natural, recyclable products made from
wood grown in sustainable forests. The manufacturing processes conform to the
environmental regulations of the country of origin.

The Random House Group Limited Reg. No. 9540009

www.randomhouse.co.uk

ISBN 0 09 941309 4

Your library is precious – Use it or lose it!

1

Alan Alexander Jones's Diary

Monday, March 4th
Today I began my hunger strike. I am a martyr. I will probably die, but if it makes my mum see sense my sacrifice won't have been in vain.

I have amazed myself with my bravery and heroic determination. I will not give in, even though this won't be a piece of cake, seeing how obsessed with food I seem to have become these last few years. E.g., I didn't begin my strike until supper-time today but am already fantasising about thick juicy steaks and heaps of crispy, golden French fries with hot apple pie and custard to follow.

But enough of that. Mind-over-matter is what this task is about, and I have a very strong mind. I take after my dad, a man of great character who is currently touring the Far East on a push-bike, having swapped his humdrum job and home for a spell of freedom and adventure. I salute him!

I know I can do this thing, so old Wimpy Walker and his stupid daughter Ella had better watch out! Wimpy might have bewitched my mum with flowers and flattery, but no way are those two going to worm their way into our house, taking over my dad's territory plus our spare bedroom which currently houses my train layout and stacks of old Beanos. Dashing their predatory hopes will give me as much satisfaction as a plateful of juicy pork bangers and mashed with rhubarb tart for afters.

In a crisis like this you expect some support from your friends, but when I told Dez and Josh my master plan they did nothing but sneer.

'If your mum wants a new partner there's nothing you can do to stop her!' they said.

Call themselves best mates! They reckon my hunger strike won't last twenty-four hours, but I'll show 'em! We aren't all as weak and spineless as those two, who couldn't stop eating even if their teeth and tongues fell out.

So here goes! I've made a determined start. I even took care not to swallow any water when I cleaned my teeth. From tomorrow, of course, I won't need to clean them any more, which is the first perk of the job.

2

Ever Diminishing Cycles

Colin Jones, father of the ravenous Alan Alexander Jones, pushed his damaged bicycle down the hill into Brimmington village. He was tired and dirty, practically penniless and thoroughly depressed. His magnificent plan to tour the world on two wheels and then sell his story to the *Sun* for a five-figure sum had brought him, after almost two years, no further than this Yorkshire village where he would now have to spend the night in a barn – if he was lucky.

All those high-falutin' ideas of freedom and adventure had long since disappeared, together with his redundancy money, on one almighty pub-crawl, two soft-hearted hand-outs and a slick-fingered pick-pocket, so he was now obliged to live on his wits. He certainly couldn't go back home, for what would his wife and son think of him if he turned up now, cowed and defeated, with nothing to show for his great adventure but a collection of souvenir beer-mats?

It was getting late. There were lights in the houses below where fortunate families would be sitting down to supper in front of the telly. That's what his wife Madge and son Alan would be doing. Did they still think kindly of him, or had they spitefully snipped his likeness out of the family snapshots and sent his Black and Decker drill to the church jumble sale? Perhaps he should have kept in touch, but how could he send cards with a Doncaster postmark when he was supposed to be in exotic places like Bali or Katmandu?

Ignorant of the fact that his wife had just decided to divorce him for desertion, Colin tried to picture himself returning home to a hero's welcome, his wallet bulging with the fruits of his endeavours. Oh, if only! He was heartily sick of freedom. Home was what he yearned for now more than anything, but he couldn't turn up there empty-handed.

He was distracted from this daydream by the sudden appearance of a lighted shop ahead of him. 'Brimmington Post Office' proclaimed the sign above its door.

Colin stopped and stared. Then, suddenly inspired, he propped his bike against a tree and moved cautiously on foot towards this new-found beacon of hope. Maybe the kind post-mistress could point him in the direction of a job. There must be farms round here which could do with a helping hand.

Unfortunately Mrs Dibbet, the Postmistress, had recently been robbed by a youth in a bala-clava mask who had threatened her with a gun and gone off with the day's takings. So when this stranger turned up, this dirty, dishevelled and shifty-looking Colin, she immediately flew into a panic and pressed the emergency button, bring-ing Constable Higgins along at the double from the house next-door-but-one.

'This might look like a sleepy village, but we're well up in the ways of technology,' Constable Higgins declared with pride as he seized Colin's arm.

Colin was about to explain, but suddenly thought it might be more sensible to get arrested. At least then he would have somewhere to spend the night. Even a prison cell was better than a barn. They would soon work out that he wasn't really a criminal.

Taking care to admit to nothing, Colin simply hinted at a life of crazy risk. 'I wish I'd stayed at home and got on with my humdrum life,' he confessed as he emptied his pockets at the sergeant's desk in the local police station, 'but you know how it is, you get restless. Wanderlust's a terrible thing. You take my advice, officer, and be content with your lot.'

The sergeant, who had a nagging wife, four children and a never-diminishing mortgage, answered only with a grunt as he led Colin away to the nearest cell.

3

Prunella Walker's Diary

Monday, March 4th

Today I began my Great Silence and sent the whole world to Coventry. From this moment I am struck dumb and won't speak another word to anyone until my dad sees sense, though I'll write him plenty of notes to make sure he knows what I'm up to. We are NOT going to live with those stupid Joneses in dreary Flumpton, even though it is only the next town and their house is supposed to be bigger than ours. I have no intention of being uprooted, and the sooner Dad realises it, the better.

So Ma Jones's old man went off on a biking holiday and never came back, sensible bloke, and now she's

divorcing him for desertion? Well, bully
for her! But there's no need for Dad to
keep telling me this tale over and over
again. He's about as understanding
and tactful as a Guess-Your-Weight
machine. This woman obviously can't
wait to get her claws into another
meal-ticket, and that Alan son of hers
sounds a proper mother's boy, totally
pathetic. I'm glad we've never met,
and I don't intend to change that
situation if I live to be a hundred.
Flumpton's a right old dump; it hasn't
even got a decent library.

I'm bound to be heading for trouble
with this silence, but who can blame
me for keeping alive my dead mum's
memory? I have made a vow that
nobody is going to take her place, and
what's wrong with that? I know I have
right on my side and that will keep me
going through thick and thin.

Mum always said I was a champion

chatterbox who only stopped talking when asleep, and not always then. So I know I have taken on a mammoth task but am sure I can do it, especially if I let off plenty of steam in this diary. There's such a thing as self-control, something Dad doesn't seem to have much of these days, and I don't see how anybody can make me speak if I refuse to. Even if they prise my jaws apart they won't get any sound out of me.

My biggest problem will be school, but even there I reckon I can make my dumbness seem like a terrible trauma for which I need lots of time off and gentle counselling. Old Verity has a degree in psychology, which I suppose is an essential requirement for any headteacher these days. She will 'Understand Me' in a big way and may even offer one-to-one home tuition to prevent me falling behind in my work. I wouldn't mind that; I reckon I could communicate with a personal tutor by means of scribbles, nods and headshakes, plus a few hand signals. I might even learn proper sign language if this looks like dragging on for a while, though I'm hoping it will all be over by Easter; they'll be scared of it getting into the papers.

One person who needs to be in the know is my best friend Lucy. We've been best friends since nursery school and it would be awful if she took this silence personally so I'm going to let her read my diary every day, making sure she's up to date with what's going on. She won't betray me, but even if disaster strikes, such as her carelessly letting my diary fall into the wrong hands, ESPECIALLY HER GOSSIPY MUM'S – (Lucy please note!!) – there's still no way anybody can force me to talk, not even her.

I'm going to put some Sellotape over my lips when I get into bed, just as a reminder for when I wake up in the morning. That's in case Dad shouts upstairs as usual and I make the mistake of answering while I'm still half asleep. I've also put notepads and pens all over the house and written SSSH! on a big sheet of card hanging on my bedroom door. It will be the first thing I see when I wake up.

Well, I guess I've thought of everything. All I have to do now is to sit back and wait for a result. I reckon it will be quite restful, not having to use my vocal cords. It might even have improved my voice when I do get it back, which will be a bonus for the Drama Club of which I am the undisputed star.

4

Alan Alexander Jones's Diary

Tuesday, March 5th

I've decided I'm going to write a handbook for hunger-strikers if I live through this – (and if I don't, perhaps whoever finds this diary can write it for me) – so I'd better keep very detailed notes. After all, this is a major campaign just as important as any military strategy so it needs to be properly planned and executed.

The main thing is to out-manoeuvre the opposition. Mum didn't half nag when I refused my breakfast this morning, though if only she knew it, nagging simply strengthens my resolve. She'd done sausages and bacon with fried bread and the smell was so delicious I couldn't help groaning. In

*the end she decided I must be ill. She
actually took my temperature, peered at
my tongue and throat and asked me
some embarrassing questions. When
she couldn't find any symptoms except
dribbling – (my mouth was watering
like the Trevi fountain) – she accused
me of looking for an excuse to cut
school, but I certainly wasn't. I couldn't
get there fast enough, being eager to
escape from the temptations of her
cooking.*

*Anyone who has ever faced the day
with a stomach like a burst balloon will
know how brave I was to run for the
school bus as usual. How was I to
know that Stuart Hayes would force me
to take a handful of his monster bag of
Chipples? Well, any campaign has its
minor setbacks, but it's the principal
enemy you need to impress, not local
yokels like Stuart Hayes.*

It wasn't too difficult to dodge school

dinner – (disgusting wormy mince and
wrinkled prunes) – and I can certainly
make better use of the money. But I
must admit that by three o'clock I was
in a state of near collapse. I decided I
should have worked myself into this
thing a bit more gently. After all, I'm a
growing lad and if I die too quickly the
advantage will be lost; Mum won't
have to watch me slowly pining away
as her guilt deepens. In fact a sudden
shock would just catapult her straight
into Wimpy Walker's arms for
consolation. So I shut myself in the
toilets and ate a Mars bar to give me
the strength to get home. This does not
constitute a failure of my plan, merely
a sensible re-appraisal of the situation.

No sooner had I entered the house
than I smelt the steak-and-kidney pie
which was cooking for supper. This
really was too much, so I went straight
out again and round to Josh's. Josh's

*mum was just serving up banana
milkshake and biscuits which I politely
refused. Her astonishment was
amazing, but not as amazing as Josh's
efforts to tempt me. I guess he has a bet
on me giving up. He even slipped a
couple of biscuits into my pocket so I
let it be known that I was thinking of
feeding the ducks in the park on the
way home.*

*I redeemed myself by going straight
up to my room when I got in. Mum
came banging on the door, of course,
saying she had something important to
tell me, but I'm not stupid; that was
just an excuse to get me to go down
and eat my supper. I told her I'd eaten
at Josh's and at long, long last she
went away. Dogged perseverance,
that's what's needed. Dig in and
consolidate your position.*

*Once I've finished writing this I shall
fall into bed with only dreams – or*

possibly nightmares – of the steak-and-kidney pie, and with the satisfaction of knowing that my first day's hunger strike has been a great success. Dad would be proud to know that I'd inherited his high-minded enterprise and courage. I keep thinking of him being fêted by some glittering Maharajah after having cycled up the highest mountain in the area and planted the Union Jack on the top. What's my effort compared to that?

5

Out of Court Proceedings

In his cell at the local police station, Colin Jones was just getting acquainted with his breakfast when Constable Higgins came to tell him it was time to go and see the magistrate.

'Haven't finished me porridge,' objected Colin.

'You can say that again!' grinned the constable, puffed up with his own wit.

But pride comes before a fall. As the constable advanced into the cell he slipped on a spilt glob of porridge. His feet flew up in front of him and his head hit the concrete floor with an almighty crack and he lay as if dead, eyes closed and face a chalky white.

Horrified at what he'd done, Colin panicked. The constable was obviously dead. He leapt over the unconscious body and dashed through the open cell door to freedom, neatly dodging the desk sergeant who was deeply absorbed in an important telephone conversation. Whizzing through the revolving doors, Colin leapt straight on to a moving bus which had barely picked up speed after leaving the last stop.

Penniless though he was, Colin's good luck held as the driver told him to sit down before he fell down and pay when he got off. To crown it all, as they reached the roundabout in nearby Dabley's town centre, the traffic lights failed and rush-hour chaos ensued. Horns hooted, drivers yelled and simmering road-rage finally boiled over. Vehicle doors began to slam as red-faced protagonists – including the bus driver – leapt out to shake their fists in one another's faces.

Relieved at Fate's obliging collaboration, Colin leapt off the bus and sped nimbly round the corner into the local railway station where he hid in a waiting room until a train came in. Not caring what its destination might be, he leapt on to it without a ticket and settled himself near the door in preparation for a hasty exit.

Long before a police chase had been set in motion, Colin was speeding anxiously northwards, not knowing where he would end up. For a good fifteen minutes he was able to sit and recover – until the ticket collector hove into view. Fortunately, by this time the train was about to stop, so Colin jumped off at a neglected and unstaffed little platform with the name of Bank End. Escaping thankfully into a leafy lane, he started out to assess the area's possibilities.

6

Prunella Walker's Diary,

Tuesday, March 5th
Got a detention from Mrs Pye for insolence when I wouldn't answer a question in class. She then wanted an apology and when I wouldn't give it she sent me to the Head. There I diplomatically burst into silent tears and old Verity, who was impatient to be on her way to a headteachers' conference, sent me home in the belief that my hormones were playing me up.

When I got home I was amazed to find that Dad was actually there with that awful Jones woman. They should both have been at work and they looked so guiltily pleased with themselves that you'd have thought they'd just bunked off school. I was nearly sick on the spot.

It turned out they'd been looking at rings.

RINGS!

Ma Jones explained hastily that Dad had offered to buy her a ring for a birthday present and she'd fancied this opal set in a circle of diamonds – (I bet she had!). She said the opal was her birth-stone. (Soft-soapstone, more like!) It was probably the most expensive ring in the shop and certainly sounded a lot better than anything Mum ever had. Unsurprisingly it had turned out too tight for her podgy finger so they'd had to leave it to be altered. With any luck no jeweller will ever be able to make it big enough.

It's three years next Friday since Mum died, but I guess I'm the only one who remembers. Dad remembers other dates all right. He said it was now a week since poor, deserted Ma J. had filed for divorce and another week to her birthday. So he felt the time was appropriate for him to make her a 'decent' present as a token of his esteem and support, as well as a celebration of their six-month-long friendship.

I know perfectly well what Dad's up to with that ring and he knows perfectly well I do.

'Madge has opted for freedom now,' he declared, avoiding my eye. 'So why shouldn't we be close friends?'

When I still didn't speak Ma J. started to look a bit uncomfortable.

'Maybe Ella doesn't like the idea of you giving me a ring,' she muttered. 'Perhaps a brooch would have been better, or a pair of gloves or something.'

Oh, yeah! The more presents the

merrier as far as she's concerned. And she knows perfectly well my name's Pru; I hate Ella – (only one step from Cinders) – which I swear she only uses to annoy me. She's even got Dad using it now. Odious woman!

'You don't get engaged with a pair of gloves,' I scribbled on the back of the *Radio Times*, proving that I knew exactly what was going on.

There was a pause before Dad gathered his wits, slapped down the *Radio Times* and declared defiantly: 'You have to understand, Ella, that Madge has been very good to me. You know perfectly well how down I was. She has cheered me up, lifted my spirits, given me something to live for and you should be just as grateful as I am. It's her birthday next week, she deserves a present, and I don't see why I shouldn't give her one. And that's all it is – a present.'

So I wrote:

'My name's PRU, which is what Mum always called me, or have you forgotten? And just bear in mind that I'm never going to speak again until you GET THE MESSAGE. YOU KNOW WHAT I MEAN!' Then I banged off to my room and locked the door.

That showed 'em!

On the whole a very satisfactory day.

7

Alan Alexander Jones's Diary

Wednesday, March 6th
Found out at breakfast that the important thing Mum had wanted to tell me last night was that Wimpy had taken her wandering round the jewellers' shops looking at rings.

'Just dress rings,' she hastened to add. 'Friendship rings if you like.' Any fool could see she was lying.

'Well, why not?' she snapped when I didn't respond. 'I do have a birthday coming up.'

Just for a moment I let a sneer disfigure my handsome face as I announced icily: 'This afternoon I'll be throwing some junk out of the garage to make room for Dad's bike when he makes his triumphal return' –

(propaganda tactic) – 'though of course I'll have to take it slowly, seeing I'm on hunger strike.'

'Hunger strike? You? Don't make me laugh!' Mum shouted as I marched indignantly to the door. Then, perhaps remembering that I hadn't eaten her last two dinners, she added suspiciously: 'You're up to something, aren't you? You've been in a mighty funny mood lately!'

Just when I thought I'd escaped she followed me out on to the doorstep in a sudden rush and shouted, nice and loud so the neighbours could hear, 'You know perfectly well your dad won't be coming back. He never had any intention of coming back, despite all those phoney promises. Why can't you accept it?'

Without so much as a backward glare I hurried out of earshot. Phoney promises indeed! She's just jealous of

Dad's achievements and fed up because he's far too busy to ring up or write boring old postcards.

Trouble was, I'd rushed off so fast that I was now twenty minutes too early for the bus. That meant I had to hang around the newsagent's behind the bus stop. It was raining so I went into the shop and pretended to look through the birthday cards until suspicious old Mrs Fowey asked me what I wanted and I had to buy a KitKat just to keep her happy.

I never noticed until today that wherever you turn there's a hoarding screaming food at you, anything from All Bran and Bumperburgers to Mr Kipling and Milk Tray. It's downright obscene, not to mention cruel to all the have-nots. Still, a steadfast campaigner cannot let himself be so easily demoralised. I got to school relatively unscathed, despite Dez ramming a

couple of Softmints into my mouth
when I yawned – (I managed to spit
them out into his blazer pocket) – and
Josh chomping noisily as he
deliberately breathed the fumes of a
bar of fruit-and-nut right in my face.

Felt very lethargic right through
Maths, though this is not unusual.
Tried to cry off P.E. with back trouble,
but didn't manage it and nearly fell off
the wall-bars with exhaustion. If I
hadn't furtively consumed the KitKat at
break I think I'd have finished up in
Intensive Care and it's too early yet.
(It's essential to plan The Right
Moment to Strike.)

Then the latest bombshell. When I
got home Mum announced that, like it
or not, I was to join her and the
Wimpy Walkers at a celebration dinner
party on Saturday night at the Linden
Tree, which is the poshest restaurant
for miles around. Five courses and

coffee, she told me pointedly, so there
was to be no nonsense about hunger
strikes.

'Celebration for what?'

'My birthday, of course, as if you
didn't know! We can't go on the actual
day because George is working late.
And this is your big change to meet
George's daughter,' she threatened.

What, the unlovely, unlovable Ella?
No way!

I haven't thought up my excuse yet,
but Mum might as well resign herself to
a table for three. Looks as if Saturday
might be my big day – a chance to
make a real impact.

8

Colin Reaches New Heights – and Depths

Back at the sleepy village of Bank End, after careful reconnoitring Colin Jones had discovered a solitary cottage half-concealed by a thick stretch of woodland. The cottage had a ladder propped against its shed and the occupants were obviously away from home. A note under a stone on the front step read: 'No milk until the 8th thank you', and today, by Colin's somewhat hazy calculations, was only the 6th, or at worst the 7th. However, the milkman must have been illiterate as there were two full bottles on the step.

Now temptation reared its ugly head. He could drink the milk at this empty house, then use the ladder to break in. Colin had never burgled a house before but there was a first time for everything and he had to admit that his needs were urgent. The police would have circulated

31

his description by now, so the first priority was a change of clothes, followed by food and cash.

He tried to convince himself that a householder in a decent area like this would be well insured, so there would be no need to feel guilty. He wouldn't take any heirlooms or things with sentimental value; just the basic necessities of life, to which every human being was surely entitled. Yet Colin surprised himself by discovering a conscience. He couldn't do it. He didn't have the right criminal attributes, whatever those might be.

In fact, he began to feel a strong compulsion to put temptation out of the way of others, too. First he moved the milk bottles round to the back of the house where they couldn't be seen from the road. Then he seized the ladder, intending to set it down under the privet hedge in the back garden.

He was just staggering round the side of the house with the ladder when a car drew up at the front gate. The owner, Miss Stringer, P.E. instructress from the local high school, was returning from a conference on Physical Pitfalls of the Teenage Years and immediately saw Colin as a housebreaker.

Before Colin realised what was happening some super-energetic and muscular creature had leapt upon him and twisted his right arm behind him in a painful lock.

9

Prunella Walker's Diary

Wednesday, March 6th

Finished up in Verity's office again.
She told me off for coming back to
school before I had 'recovered'. I was
distracting the rest of the class, she
said, and wouldn't I please confide in
her what the matter was, even if I
needed to write it down? I just hung
my head and shook it. I thought she
was going to shake ME! But she
pulled herself together and admitted
that she had been a teenager once
herself – (wonders never cease!) –
and understood the pressures. She
even offered me a double-strength
Marks and Sparks tissue and a
sympathetic pat on the shoulder. If the
Chair of Governors hadn't turned up

with a complaint about parking spaces just then I might easily have caved in.

BUT I DIDN'T.

Got home to news of some dinner party those two have cooked up for Saturday night, at the Linden Tree of all places. I've always wanted to eat somewhere posh like that, but if they think I'm going along to be paired off with her idiot son they've another think coming. I never want to set eyes on him as long as I live.

Decided I'm going to talk to Lucy after all, but only when we're entirely alone. She'll be sworn to secrecy, of course, but I have to talk to somebody; this silence is driving me mad. Besides, I've decided I don't want her to read my diary after all. It might inhibit some of the entries I want to make. I can see me getting down to some very strong language and raw emotions before this business is over.

10

Alan Alexander Jones's Diary

Saturday, March 9th

Mum sent me to the supermarket for the weekend shopping as usual, though I admit it nearly killed me, pushing that great heavy trolley up and down the aisles on an empty stomach. A good thing some shopper had left an over-ripe banana behind in one, and also that it was the store demonstrator's day for offering free samples of mock-turtle soup. Very nourishing – I had six. (Well, finds and freebies don't count; a good campaigner will seize any opportunity to help his cause.)

Needed a rest before I staggered to the bus stop with my three heavy bags, so I sat on a seat at the taxi pick-up point to marshal my strength. There I

was, *brooding about tonight's fiasco
and polishing up my excuse, when this
girl came and sat down on the next
seat. Brunette, not bad-looking,
wearing a red leather jacket and jeans
and carrying nearly as much shopping
as I was.*

*She looked pale and interesting – a
bit miserable as a matter of fact – so I
shuffled along a bit and asked her if
she was waiting for a taxi. She nodded
her head and her long, shiny hair
bobbed about like a t.v. shampoo ad.
Very fetching!*

*I began chatting her up, but she
didn't seem very forthcoming. She
seemed to communicate by nods and
shrugs. Probably her mum tells her
never to talk to strangers. I could see I
was probably wasting my time, but
couldn't resist dropping a hint that I
usually spent my Saturday evenings
down at the Snazzy Snack Bar from*

about 8 p.m. Then, playing it cool, I
got up and walked away, as casually as
I could with all that shopping. It
doesn't do to look too eager, but I
couldn't help thinking that treating her
to a Snazzy Special would be a good
alternative to this dinner party from
hell with the Wimps.

I'd hardly unpacked the shopping
before Mum started chivvying me to get
ready for the Big Night.

'Have a shower and wash your hair.
And wear something decent; I want you
to look presentable for once,' she
nagged.

I got ready all right, but not for the
big night she had in mind. I even
washed behind my ears and cleaned my
shoes just in case my shy brunette
turned up.

'And I don't want any nonsense
about hunger strikes,' Mum nattered
on. 'Just you look as though you're

enjoying this expensive dinner, and remember your manners. Eat nicely and smile; even you can manage that if you put your mind to it. Afterwards don't forget to say thank you to George, and be specially nice to young Ella. She's about your age, so you should have plenty in common.'

(Oh yeah! Like hatred? Disgust? Black boredom? Boiling rage?)

I noticed Mum had bought herself an expensive new number and some extra make-up, so I managed to sneak out the back way while she was still having a one-to-one with the mirror. I know there'll be hell to pay tomorrow when she catches up with me. But that's tomorrow.

By the time I got to the Snazzy I was in such a state I didn't care who was there. I'd convinced myself that the brunette certainly wouldn't be; she was way out of my league, but with a bit of

luck I might spot Dez or Josh. What I
wanted mostly was a bit of distraction
– something to cheer me up, or failing
that, some peace and quiet in which to
nurse my wounds and my seriously
growling stomach. But the minute I
opened the door I saw her – my
mystery girl, my Tesco vision, sitting by
herself in a corner.

By herself!

A pale face loomed above that bright
red jacket, and her face broke into a
very faint (but unmistakable) smile as
she spotted me coming in. Dazed but
elated, I ordered two Snazzy Specials
and one chocolate éclair and made it
to her table in three strides.

'Aren't you having one?' she
muttered as I pushed the éclair towards
her. Downing the Snazzy Special
greedily, I told her I was on hunger
strike but she obviously thought I was a
failed comedian.

'Oh, sure!' Staring pointedly at my empty glass, she gave a sarky (but melodious) laugh. I didn't mind; it improved her looks even more.

'It's true, only I don't want to die too quickly so I'm pacing myself.'

I won't record her reply to this, but eventually she added, through the second bite of the éclair, 'Didn't you wonder why I never spoke to you at lunch-time?'

'Didn't you?' I retorted coolly.

Then she told me she'd got into the habit of not speaking because she'd been sending someone to Coventry.

'Well, a lot of people actually. As a matter of fact I don't speak at all these days,' she said, 'unless I'm well away from home and with people who hardly know me.'

(Was I supposed to take that as a compliment?)

'You do what you think best,' I told

her. 'Matters of principle are never easy. That's what got me into my hunger strike.'

Before long we were getting on like a stir-fry and I'd already decided this was the girl for me. She had courage, strength of will and similar principles which would do nicely for a start.

She said her name was Pru, which I guessed was short for Prudence. A moral name; I like it. Has a lot more dignity than Wimpy's Ella, which could only be telescopic for 'umbrella'.

We began to exchange dark hints about our tragic lives. She was mad at her dad for some reason – (she wouldn't say what) – but not half as mad as I was at my mum. What we did have in common was that we were both trying to teach our Olds a lesson. A five-star bond! A pity she lives in Preesall, a good bus-ride away, but at

*least she does her shopping at
Flumpton Tesco.*

*The evening was a big improvement
on any would-be family get-together,
five courses or not. In fact, that
particular problem began to shrink so
swiftly into insignificance that I ordered
a chocolate éclair after all. It was truly
delicious.*

11

Striking the Right Note at Last

In a bizarre sort of way Colin Jones's luck still held, for his first night on remand in Wiltways gaol – (a different matter altogether from a night in the village lock-up) – was enlivened by the visit of the Meritone String Quartet.

Straight after supper, prisoners were assembled in the gym where stacking-chairs had been laid out in rows, playing havoc with the highly-polished floor.

The over-dressed and over-eager group played Mozart selections on violins, viola and 'cello in a vain attempt to soothe the savage breast. Well, perhaps not entirely vain; this was certainly better than sitting in a cell twiddling your thumbs and suffering from passive smoking.

But after the interval things took a turn for the better. One violinist laid aside his instrument, produced a guitar and plunged into a medley of the jolliest tunes Colin had ever heard.

Colin was entranced. This was more like it!

This was something really worth listening to – something he'd like to have a go at himself! This idle strumming looked so easy, too. He could pick it up in no time.

This was the first occasion in his life on which the true creative urge had been stirred in Colin. Making up for lost time, it swept him literally off his feet as he leapt to applaud and was pushed back into his seat by a vigilant warder.

But the bug had bitten hard. Two days later Colin was practising on an old guitar from the Occupational Therapy room, and convincing himself that he had discovered a talent he would never have believed existed. Why, he could turn out to be another Elvis Presley! Maybe it was Fate which had led him to gaol in order to fulfil his true destiny. Maybe it was not too late to acquire fame and fortune and to impress his family after all!

12

Prunella Walker's Diary

Sunday, March 10th

Yesterday started badly. On my way to the supermarket I called for Lucy and told her I could talk to her again after all, but she decided to take the huff and refused to talk to ME. She actually slammed the door in my face and I suppose I can't blame her after my recent performance. Still, it's a pretty desperate state of affairs; I have to talk to somebody or I'll go completely bonkers.

Things did improve after that, though. Not only did I manage to dodge this dire dinner party, but I actually found somebody I COULD talk to. Such a relief, as I was getting really suicidal, never having realised what a blessing simple, ordinary speech could be.

I met this boy at the supermarket called Alex. It turns out he also has the hated surname of Jones, but that's so common I've decided not to hold it against him...nor the fact that he goes to Flumpton Comprehensive.

He's tall, fairly blond and quite dishy except that he's a bit thin. I met him again in the evening at the Snazzy – accidentally on purpose! – and he told me he was on hunger strike, but of course I knew that was just his excuse for his lack of physique; boys are over-sensitive about these things. He ate plenty there and then, I must say! Chocolate éclairs, ice creams, Yorkie bars, Snazzy Specials, you name it! I bet he feels pretty sick today.

Spotted Lucy walking her dog in the park this morning but she pretended she hadn't seen me. Maybe she'd heard something about Alex and was green with jealousy, since Adam Riley's just dumped her for a girl in 7B. Anyway, she wouldn't even glance in my direction which serves me right, I suppose, for the way I've been behaving.

By the time I got home I'd done quite a bit of thinking and was wondering if I'd taken things too far. Perhaps I ought to start talking again. I'm in so much trouble one way and another that it would be a relief to give in. But then Dad pitched into me about not turning up at the Linden Tree last night. Said I'd shown him up, let him down, insulted his woman and ruined the whole evening, and where had I been anyway? He got quite fierce, so I decided not to give in after all. Scribbled 'Switch off, Dad!' on the edge of the electricity bill and waved it under his nose. Serves him jolly well right!

13

Alan Alexander Jones's Diary

Sunday, March 10th

Felt really sick this morning so stayed in bed. Probably wolfed down too much too quickly last night on a seriously empty stomach, but I'd reasoned that if Pru could break her silence just for me, then I could break my fast just for her. After all, she's not involved in my problem so why should she suffer the consequences? It doesn't mean I've given up the battle. As far as Mum's concerned I'm still on strike.

No peace for the wicked, though; Mum came barging into the bedroom without knocking, demanding to know where I'd been last night and why I'd shown her up. When I said how rotten I felt she thought I was just shamming to keep myself out of trouble. I got no sympathy whatsoever until I actually threw up all over the duvet.

Still, once Mum had cleaned me up and sorted me out I was able to lie there and daydream about Prudence. She IS the girl of my dreams, no doubt about it. I just wonder why she won't tell me her surname. She says it's because she's in trouble at school (Preesall High) for not speaking. She wants to keep this up but she has to be consistent. If anybody finds out that she talks to me and that she's not suffering some terrible trauma after all, she'll be in even worse trouble.

Feeling slightly better, I was just deciding to get up when I heard voices on the stairs. To my utter amazement Mum marched in with the doctor! On a Sunday, too; he must have thought it was a dire emergency. Before I could protest that there was nothing wrong with me Mum began telling him that I was suffering from anorexia or bulimia or both and that she wanted something done about it before it was too late.

There followed a humiliating session of pokes and prods and questions, after which the doctor straightened up and declared there was nothing wrong with me that a bit of fresh air, exercise and sensible diet wouldn't cure.

'But he reckons he's on hunger strike,' Mum insisted.

'Not this lad,' retorted the doctor, briskly gathering his things together and departing. 'Just the opposite, I'd say.'

Well, that did it! After she'd shown him out Mum came back upstairs to do battle, the outcome being that I spent the whole afternoon cleaning the windows and washing her car.

14

Striking the Wrong Note

The occupational therapist at Wiltways, a generous-hearted man known chummily as Pete, felt sorry for Colin Jones, the docile prisoner with the bewildered, hangdog look. Colin was surely no hardened criminal but a mere pawn in Fate's uncompromising hand; a victim – (as Colin himself shyly insisted he was) – of a series of unfortunate misunderstandings. Colin looked totally out of place among these other great, hulking bullies. Furthermore, in his very first week he had already proved himself a man of sensitivity, the first Wiltways prisoner ever to show an interest in music – a subject which was Pete's abiding passion.

When Colin asked to borrow the old guitar which Pete had left lying temptingly around, Pete felt as though his mammoth efforts at Wiltways had not been entirely in vain after all.

Not only did he lend Colin the guitar plus a simple 'Teach Yourself' manual, but he wangled permission from the Governor for Colin to practise for one hour a day in a corner of the workroom.

Unfortunately, the group sharing this room with Colin at this time included an evil-tempered couple known as Lurcher and Fryup, neither of whom had any more love of music than a moth trapped in a drum. No sooner did Colin strike the first chord at the appointed hour than these two set upon him and tried to snatch the guitar away. But Colin was tougher than he looked, and quite determined on his brilliant dream-future. He held on tightly to his instrument, managed to wrench it away then swung round and whacked Fryup accidentally over the head with it. Fryup collapsed in a pool of blood, Lurcher set upon Colin yelling blue murder and all over the prison bells began to ring.

15

Alan Alexander Jones's Diary

Monday, March 11th
Suddenly realised during Chemistry that Prudence must go to the same school as Wimpy Ella. There's only one secondary school in Preesall, namely Preesall High. Anybody who doesn't go there gets bussed to our place. Wish I'd thought to get P's number, then I could have rung her tonight and asked her what the wimp was like. Never mind; we're meeting at Preesall McDonald's tomorrow (my turn for the bus-ride) so all will be well.

Had a big confrontation with Mum when she got home from work. She said the doctor's visit on Sunday was the biggest humiliation of her life and she would never be able to face him again.

*Furthermore, if there was any more
nonsense about pretend hunger strikes
she'd force-feed me like they did with
the suffragettes.*

*I pointed out that a hunger strike
was only one form of protest. There
were plenty of others she might like
even less, such as not speaking ever
again – (sorry, Pru!) – or running
away to sea.*

*What was I protesting about? she
demanded, as if she didn't know. But it
was time we put our cards on the table
so I dealt mine face-up.*

*'This is OUR home,' I declared. 'MY
home! DAD's home! I don't want it
overrun by strangers and their grotty
belongings. I'm entitled to my privacy
and space. I'm entitled to have a say
in my future...' etc., etc. I got quite
animated, waved my arms about and
said a lot more than I meant to.*

I'll give Mum her due, she heard me

*out without interrupting. But then she
did a terrible thing. She burst into
tears. That really threw me; I didn't
know what to do. I'd only ever seen her
cry twice before – once at her mum's
funeral and once on that fateful day
when she watched Dad pedalling off
down the drive.*

*For a while I stood there looking
helpless while she sobbed something
about this being her last chance of
happiness, her very last; then I bolted
into the kitchen to fetch her a box of
tissues. After a bit I went all soft and
put my arm round her. Then I heard
myself promising that of course I
wouldn't do anything daft like running
away to sea, I hadn't meant a word of
it. But I was careful not to say I
wouldn't re-start my hunger strike. It
won't be as easy now, though. It isn't
fair, the way women use tears to soften
us up. If I cried, I'd just be told to grow
up and stop being such a baby.*

16

Murder Most Foul

'Dead?' cried Pete, turning white and floppy as half-whipped cream. 'But he can't be! It's not possible to kill someone with a non-electric guitar!'

'Don't you believe it!' retorted the warder, happy to shock that soft-hearted occupational therapist who was far too pally with the prisoners. 'And you're in this up to your neck, lending out lethal weapons to all and sundry.'

The warder knew perfectly well that the overweight and junk-fed Fryup had died of a heart attack, though this had quite likely been brought on by Colin's blow. All the same, it would do Pete good to worry, since he'd been daft enough to lend the guitar in the first place. He must have known the noise a learner makes on any instrument would be enough to start a riot in a place like that.

'W-what happens now?'

'Who knows?' shrugged the warder. 'Pity they did away with capital punishment!'

Pete was appalled. Was this really all his fault? He felt that no single moment in his life could ever be as terrible as this. Yet there were other terrible moments in store. No sooner had he stepped outside the prison that night on his guilt-wracked way home than he was accosted by an eager group of journalists, for bad news travels fast.

As a result, next morning's papers carried jokey banner headlines such as: LAST CHORD; DEATH TO SOME TUNE; OBLITERATIONAL THERAPY etc., each accompanied by grossly exaggerated write-ups, photographs of a cowering Pete and repeated mentions of the now notorious Colin.

On her way to work Mrs Jones bought her usual copy of the *Sun*, although she had long since ceased to search its pages for Colin's name and all that promised glory. Yet as often happens, once you stop looking for something you find it. Today there was Colin's name, right in front of her eyes. Not the glory, though; in fact, quite the opposite.

In growing horror, Mrs Jones absorbed fact

after dreadful fact. Not only had her husband abandoned his world cycling tour but he had never even left the country. Moreover, he'd turned out to be a thief, a housebreaker, a common criminal. No; worse than that! He was a killer!

Weak with shock, the poor woman staggered back home, sank into a chair and gazed blankly at the wall in front of her. For almost half an hour she made no move, while her tortured brain struggled to come to terms with these dreadful truths. Oh, the shame of it all! And George – what on earth was George going to think? She felt as if her whole world had turned suddenly upside down.

17

Prunella Walker's Diary

Tuesday, 12th March

It's worked! Dad has abandoned his diabolical plan to move in with Ma Jones. I can hardly believe it! They had some sort of a bust-up tonight via this forty-minute telephone conversation in which Dad really let rip. I couldn't hear the nitty-gritty as I'd been banished to my room, but there's plenty to be gleaned from tone of voice if you hang far enough over the banister. Besides, he announced afterwards in clipped and bitter phrases that it was all over and no doubt I'd be pleased.

That was his way of acknowledging my responsibility for the whole thing, and needless to say I do take all the credit. My silence has evidently worn him down. So it's all been worth-while, even the frostiness with Lucy, which I'll soon thaw out now. I can SPEAK! The relief is wonderful!

18

Alan Alexander Jones's Diary

Tuesday, 12th March
*Success at last! And judging from my
vanishing biceps, not a moment too
soon.*

*Tonight Mum and Wimpy Walker had
this great bust-up on the 'phone in
which Mum kept saying things like 'No
reason; I just know now that it won't
work', and 'No; I won't ever change
my mind. Circumstances are different
now.' Then she burst into tears again,
but I refuse to feel guilty. My hunger
strike has saved her from a fate worse
than death. Proudly I see that she does
value my life and happiness after all,
and that she's not forgotten Dad. Now,
hurray! I need never meet the limp,
unlovely Ella – and best of all, I can*

stuff myself with heaps of luscious nosh! This is a red-letter day and no mistake! Can't wait to tell Prudence when I meet her after school tomorrow.

Wish I could get in touch with Dad, though. This would be the ideal moment for him to come home. Even if he's as far away as Australia he could take to the air and be back in forty-eight hours at most.

19

Prunella Walker's Diary

Wednesday, 20th March

Dad's really upset. I hate to see him
like this. It's as if he's lost all will to live
and I'm getting extremely worried.

This last week, since he broke up
with Ma Jones, has been awful. He's
not been to work or ventured outside
the house at all, not even to the pub.
Maybe I under-estimated how much
he needed a bit of feminine company.
He's looked so ill that I tried to
persuade him to go to the doctor's but
he wouldn't even do that.

I've been so busy trying to cheer
him up that I've not even had time to
write my diary. But all my efforts have
been in vain. He's even lost interest in
telly football and has started smoking

again after more than six years. He just sits and stares into space which is very unnerving. So now I've decided that I'll have to do something about it since I guess it's really all my fault for making such a fuss.

What's needed is another woman friend livelier and more attractive than Ma Jones. Somebody to take him out of himself; a cheerful, caring sort who's not going to dump him without warning just when he's grown interested and is on the verge of getting engaged.

I've discussed this with Alex and he thinks I'm right, but where do I start looking? I did consider putting an ad. in the Lonely Hearts column of the local paper, but Alex said that would just be asking for trouble. Goodness knows who might turn up, a psycho or even a really vicious criminal type. He looked ever so weird when he said

that, as though he'd got some first-
hand experience. Maybe he's having
trouble with one of his relatives, a
shop-lifting auntie or something. He's
right though, I can't just leave it to
blind chance.

So I've decided to make a list of all
the things Dad reckoned he admired in
Ma Jones, which will help me to find a
substitute. He used to be forever
checking over her good qualities like
some vital shopping-list, so it wasn't
difficult. It seems she was big on
patience, intelligence, a fine sense of
humour, excellent cooking skills, good
dress sense, etc., etc. I'll set half the
class on to it tomorrow. Surely
between all our relatives and
neighbours we can come up with
somebody who fits the bill.

20

Alan Alexander Jones's Diary

Wednesday, 20th March

I've still not recovered from the shock. In fact, my hand's shaking even now, as I make my first diary entry for a week.

I tried hard to convince myself that you couldn't always believe what you read in the papers. This wasn't MY dad; there were millions of Joneses in the world. But then the photograph appeared and there was no way I could dodge the issue after that. My dad is a cheat and a deceiver; a housebreaker; a criminal; a total disaster. MY DAD!

When you've looked up to someone all your life this is a hard blow to take. You look for excuses. Could he have been falsely accused? But there were so many wrongdoings listed that they

couldn't all be mistakes. Besides, Mum
says she's not a bit surprised. He was
always like that: weak-willed, work-
shy, impulsive, utterly selfish and full of
daft ideas. Well, I must admit she was
always hinting as much but I chose
never to believe her.

Now I can hardly bear to think of all
the lies he told us. Some world cycling
tour – he never even left the country!
And to think I went on hunger strike on
his account! I could have killed myself
all for nothing. (Good sub-title for the
hunger-strikers' handbook!) I know it
was partly about the Wimpy Walkers as
well, but only because I thought they
were trying to steal his place.

I've actually ended up feeling sorry
for Mum. On top of all this shame and
humiliation I'm beginning to suspect
she's been ditched by Wimpy. I
overheard the bust-up, and at first I
thought it was down to me and my

hunger strike, but now I'm starting to wonder. I guess he found out about Dad and took flight, the rotten coward. A week ago I'd have found this a cause for rejoicing, but now I think it's very badly timed. Mum desperately needs cheering up and I'm the one who'll have to sort things out for her.

I've come to the sad conclusion that Mum's entirely right to go for a divorce now, but she needs someone besides me to look after her. Someone to make a fuss of her and give her a good time, which apparently Dad never did.

Honestly, parents are a big responsibility. I guess we never stop worrying about them all our lives. Goodness knows what becomes of the grown-ups who have no kids to sort them out.

But mercifully, Mum has me and I won't be satisfied until I've thought of a way to put the zing back in her life.

So I've decided to make a list of all the good qualities she used to keep on saying she'd found in Wimpy Walker. Courtesy, honesty, generosity, intelligence, a good sense of fun, etc. Surely there's somebody somewhere who can match up to this. I'll get Dez and Josh on to it. Dez has at least one bachelor uncle and there's a widower next door to Josh who keeps on cadging meals off them because he can't cook. One whiff of Mum's chicken casserole and he'd be hooked. I bet we'll have this sorted by the weekend.

21

A New Leaf – or Maybe a Whole New Book

Colin Jones was about to regain his freedom. Fryup's death had been confirmed as due to natural causes after all, and the other misunderstandings had at last been sorted out.

This was his new opportunity, then. With a clean slate and a clear conscience he could now stride forward into a better life. The prison occupational therapist, a decent bloke if ever there was one, had fixed Colin up with a job in a music shop, dusting the instruments, making the tea and running errands. He would actually be earning money, so he could save up for his own guitar – (probably get one at a discount price through working in the shop) – and shoot to rapid fame via some television programme like 'Opportunity Knocks'. That would stun his family, and no mistake! Just wait till they saw his likeness on the box!

22

Prunella Walker's Diary

Thursday, 21st March

Bumped into Alex at the supermarket after school. He looked so miserable I dragged him into the snack bar. We'd hardly sat down when he started pouring out his troubles. Apparently his mum's great love affair has just gone down the pan and she's dying of a broken heart. He seems to think it's all his fault because he made it plain he hated this bloke, who certainly does sound like a nasty piece of goods. Alan asked his friends to rally round, looking for a substitute, but they've all refused to help him.

I told him I understood perfectly, being in more or less the same position. That didn't seem to cheer him up, though. In fact, I don't think he was even listening when I tried bringing him up to date on MY problem. I'm beginning to think he's very self-centred and pathetic, always feeling sorry for himself. I'm not sure if I want to see him again. I've got enough to worry about as it is.

23

Alan Alexander Jones's Diary

Friday, 22nd March
The solution struck me like a bullet in the middle of Maths!

Pru's been telling me how depressed her dad is after breaking off a long-standing friendship with some really awful, unsuitable woman. Of course Pru's wanting to help him get over that, just as I'm wanting to help Mum. So I suddenly thought – it's obvious! Why don't we work together? Q.E.D. I don't know why we didn't think of it sooner.

Wasn't it Einstein who said the simplest solutions for great problems are usually the best? All we have to do is to introduce our folks to one another and take it from there. From what Pru says about her dad, he has all the qualities Mum's looking for, and as for his ideal woman, it fits Mum to a T. We can't lose!

By break-time I had it all worked out. I'll explain to Mum that I've got a new girlfriend I'd like her to meet, and that to compensate for not turning up at the Linden Tree last time I'd like this meeting to take place there, my treat. (I'll have to borrow the cash from Josh but he owes me anyway, and Mum will be only too glad to pay off the debt when she realises what it was all in aid of.) Pru and I will make the introductions and ensure the meal gets off to a good start, then we'll think up some excuse to make ourselves scarce while the two of them get to know each other.

So I've sent a note to Pru via one of Josh's ex's who goes to her school. I've asked her to meet me after school tonight when I hope to tell her my plan.

I'm so certain she'll love it that I've already booked a table for four at the Linden Tree for this coming Saturday night. And this time I'll turn up willingly, in my best gear and with a ravenous appetite.